Can Kittens Take a Catnap?

by Claire Palfreman-Bunker

Illustrated by Adam Relf

SCHOLASTIC INC.

New York Toronto London Auckland Sydney
Mexico City New Delhi Hong Kong Buenos Aires

To my favorite animal lovers,
Ian and Grace
—C.B.

ISBN 13: 978-0-545-02595-9
ISBN 10: 0-545-02595-8

Text copyright © 2007 by Scholastic Inc.
Illustration copyright © 2007 by Adam Relf

12 11 10 9 8 7 6 5 4 3 2 1   7 8 9 10 11 12/0

Printed in the U.S.A.
First printing, October 2007

Book design by Jennifer Rinaldi Windau

If kittens take a catnap
curled up in a ball,

do foals take a horsenap when sleeping in the stall?

Can goslings take a goosenap huddled in the nest?

Will fawns take a deernap when lying down to rest?

Could bunnies take a rabbitnap
in fields with each other?

Does a puppy take a dognap
sprawled upon his brother?

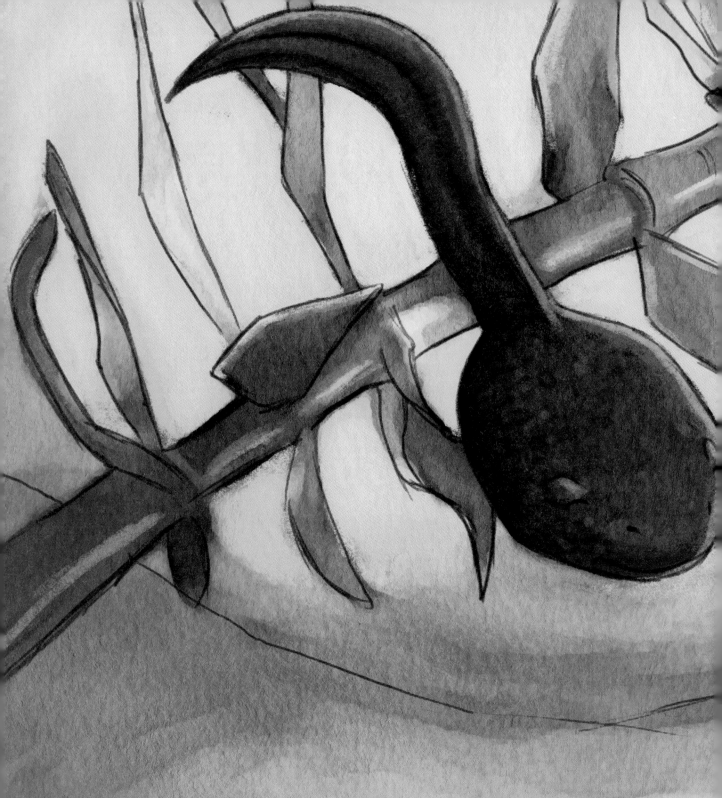

Would tadpoles take a frognap
when they go to sleep?

Can lambs take a sheepnap
as they are counting sheep?

Do piglets take a pignap buried in the mud?

Would calves take a cownap
after chewing on their cud?

Should cygnets take a swannap
while floating on the stream?

**Do joeys take a kangaroonap
tucked in a pouch to dream?**

Does a cub take a bearnap
through the winter days?

Will kids take a goatnap
in the meadow where they graze?

Should hatchlings take a turtlenap sunning on a rock?

Could ducklings take a ducknap
nestled with the flock?

So if kittens take a catnap
curled up in a ball . . .

. . . why won't my
baby brother
take a nap at all?